A Note to Parents

Welcome to REAL KIDS READERS, a series of phonics-based books for children who are beginning to read. In the classroom, educators use phonics to teach children how to sound out unfa   reading skills. A   force and buil   the same ba   l.

Of cour   reader is to ma   do that, too. Wit   he books e   sign and spa   t help new rea   enter-tain you

REAL KI   ct levels to   ace.

*   to read.
*   p.
*   own.

A contr   level. Repetition, rhyme, and humor help increase word skills. Because children can understand the words and follow the stories, they quickly develop confidence. They go back to each book again and again, increasing their proficiency and sense of accomplishment, until they're ready to move on to the next level. The result is a rich and rewarding experience that will help them develop a lifelong love of reading.

For my pal Katie Gao
—M. L.

Special thanks to
Grandma Mary Giurlando for creating Al,
and to Lands' End, Dodgeville, WI, for supplying clothing.

Produced by DWAI / Seventeenth Street Productions, Inc.

Library of Congress Cataloging-in-Publication Data

Leonard, Marcia.
  My Pal Al / by Marcia Leonard ; photography by Dorothy Handelman.
      p.   cm. — (Real kids readers. Level 1)
  Summary: A child describes the special relationship shared with a cuddly red stuffed toy.
  ISBN 0-7613-2001-6 (lib. bdg.). — ISBN 0-7613-2026-1 (pbk.)
  [1. Toys—Fiction. 2. Stories in rhyme.] I. Handelman, Dorothy, ill. II. Title. III. Series.
PZ8.3.L54925My 1998
[E]—dc21   97-40289
                                                                          CIP
                                                                          AC

pbk: 10 9 8 7 6 5 4 3 2 1
lib: 10 9 8 7 6 5 4 3 2 1

My Pal Al

Marcia Leonard

Photographs by **Dorothy Handelman**

M

The Millbrook Press

Brookfield, Connecticut

Al is my pal.

His fur is red.

He likes to sit up
on my bed.

He is not big.

He is not small.

He is not fat
or flat or tall.

15

He does not bark.

He does not purr.

But I can pat
his soft red fur.

I sing to him.

23

We skip and hop.

We run and jump.
We do not stop.

Our days are fun
and full of fizz.

Al is my pal,
and I am his.

Reading with Your Child

1. Try to read with your child at least twenty minutes each day, as part of your regular routine.
2. Keep your child's books in one convenient, cozy reading spot.
3. Read and familiarize yourself with the Phonic Guidelines below.
4. Ask your child to read *My Pal Al* out loud. If he or she has difficulty with a word:
     - Help him or her decode the word phonetically. (Say, "Try to sound it out.")
     - Encourage him or her to use picture clues. (Say, "What does the picture show?")
     - Ask him or her to use context clues. (Say, "What would make sense?")
5. If your child still doesn't "get" the word, tell him or her what it is. Don't wait for frustration to build.
6. Praise your beginning reader. With your enthusiasm and encouragement, your child will go from one success to the next.

Phonic Guidelines

Use the following guidelines to help your child read the words in *My Pal Al*.

Short Vowels
When two consonants surround a vowel, the sound of the vowel is usually short. This means you pronounce *a* as in apple, *e* as in egg, *i* as in igloo, *o* as in octopus, and *u* as in umbrella. Short-vowel words in this story include: *bed, big, but, can, fat, fun, him, his, hop, not, pal, pat, red, run, sit.*

Short-Vowel Words with Beginning Consonant Blends
When two different consonants begin a word, they usually blend to make a combined sound. Words in this story with beginning consonant blends include: *flat, skip, stop.*

Short-Vowel Words with Ending Consonant Blends
When two different consonants end a word, they usually blend to make a combined sound. Words in this story with ending consonant blends include: *jump, sing, soft.*

R-Controlled Vowels
When a vowel is followed by the letter *r*, its sound is changed by the *r*. Words in this story with *r*-controlled vowels include: *bark, fur, purr.*

Double Consonants
When two identical consonants appear side by side, one of them is silent. Double-consonant words in this story include: *fizz, full,* and words in the *all* family: *small, tall.*

Sight Words
Sight words are those words that a reader must learn to recognize immediately—by sight—instead of by sounding them out. They occur with high frequency in easy texts. Sight words not included in the above categories are: *am, and, are, days, do, does, he, I, is, likes, my, of, on, our, to, up, we.*